THE BUNNY PLAY

THE BUNNY PLAY

WRITTEN AND ILLUSTRATED BY

LOREEN LEEDY

HOLIDAY HOUSE · NEW YORK

For Margery

Library of Congress Cataloging-in-Publication Data

Leedy, Loreen.
The bunny play.

SUMMARY: When the bunnies decide to put on a musical
stage version of Little Red Riding Hood, they all work
hard in the various areas of acting, directing, set
design, publicity, and costumes.
[1. Theater—Fiction. 2. Rabbits—Fiction]
I. Title.
PZ7.L51524Bu 1988   [E]   87-17793
ISBN 0-8234-0679-2

The bunnies hop to a meeting in the garden.
They want to put on a musical play
that tells the story of Little Red Riding Hood.
They pick a director to be in charge.

There is a job for every bunny.
Some want to act, sing, and dance.
Others want to build scenery
or make costumes
or play in the band.
The bunnies choose what they want to do.

LITTLE R. R. HOOD
Sign up for:
scenery   costumes
Nan   Li
Bun
posters   lighting
Beep
props   makeup
Lin   Karen
TRYOUTS - Saturday
musicians:
1:00 1:30 2:00 3:00
sven
actors:
1:00 1:30 2:00 2:30 3:00
Harrison   Bob

Everybody needs a script
so the actors can learn their lines
and the workers can figure out what needs to be done.

The director calls for tryouts.
He wants to see how well each bunny can act, sing, and dance.

After watching them all,
the director picks the best performers for the five roles:
Little Red Riding Hood, her Mother, her Grandma, the Woodcutter,
and the Wolf.

Rehearsals begin.
The five actors start to act out the story,
and the director tells them where to move on the stage.

The actors also practice singing and dancing
because they must know every note and every step by heart.

Meanwhile, the other bunnies have work to do, too.
The conductor leads the band as they rehearse the music.

A few bunnies make posters to announce the show
and hang them up around the garden.
They also make programs and tickets.

One group sews the costumes:
Little Red's cape, Mother's long dress, Grandma's flannel nightie,
the Woodcutter's hat, and a furry gray suit for the Wolf.

Another group collects the props:
Little Red's basket and napkin, the Woodcutter's ax,
and Grandma's hot-water bottle.

Several bunnies work on the scenery.
They saw and hammer and paint to make houses and trees.

This bunny is putting up lights
that will shine down on the stage.

During the dress rehearsal,
everything comes together for the first time.
The bunnies run through the play from beginning to end,
complete with music, scenery, lights, costumes, makeup, and props.
The stage manager makes sure that everything
and everybody is in place.

At last it is opening night.
In the dressing room,
the actors get ready to go on the stage.

All of the bunnies are excited, and a little nervous.
Outside, the audience is waiting eagerly for the show to begin.

The music starts, the curtain opens,
and Little Red Riding Hood is on her way
to Grandma's house.

She sings a song . . .

and meets the Wolf . . .

and they do a dance.

Then the Wolf tricks Little Red. He tells her to pick flowers,
but he runs ahead. The curtain closes, and the scenery is changed.

The Wolf pretends to be Little Red Riding Hood, and gets into Grandma's house. Grandma faints, and the Wolf hides her underneath the bed. He puts on her nightcap, and climbs under the covers.

Little Red arrives and says, "My, what big EARS you have, Grandma!"
"The better to HEAR you with, my dear," replies the Wolf.
"And my, what big EYES you have, Grandma!"
"The better to SEE you with, my dear!"

Then Little Red says, "My, what big TEETH you have, Grandma!"
And the Wolf shouts, "The better to EAT you with, my dear!"
Little Red Riding Hood screams!

The Woodcutter rushes in and struggles with the Wolf. At last,
the Wolf lies dead, and Little Red and Grandma are saved.

The play is over.
The audience loved it and claps loudly.
All of the actors come out to take their bows.
The play is a success!

GLOSSARY

ACTOR: a performer who plays a character in a play.

AUDIENCE: the people who watch a play.

CONDUCTOR: the leader of the musicians and singers.

DIRECTOR: the person in charge of a play.

DRESS REHEARSAL: a final rehearsal with costumes, makeup, scenery, lighting, and props.

DRESSING ROOM: the area in which actors put on their costumes and makeup.

LINES: the words spoken by actors in a play.

MAKEUP: the powder, lipstick, eyeshadow and so on that actors wear on stage.

MUSICAL: a play with songs and dances.

PERFORMANCE: the acting out of a play in front of an audience.

PLAY: a story that is acted out.

PROP: an object used in a play (not costumes or scenery).

REHEARSAL: a practice time for actors and musicians.

ROLE: the part played by an actor.

SCENERY: trees, houses, or other items on stage that create the setting.

SCRIPT: the printed words of a play.

STAGE: the area where actors perform.

STAGE MANAGER: the person in charge of the stage area during a performance.

TRYOUT: the chance for an actor to show his skill in front of a director in order to get a part.